Feyesper
and the
Red Shoes

Written by

Reynaldo Encina Jopé

Illustrations by Floyd Ryan S. Yamyamin

LifeRich Publishing is a registered trademark of The Reader's Digest Association, Inc.

This is a work of fiction. All of the characters, names, incidents, organizations, and dialogue in this novel are either the products of the author's imagination or are used fictitiously.

LifeRich Publishing books may be ordered through booksellers or by contacting:

LifeRich Publishing
1663 Liberty Drive
Bloomington, IN 47403
www.liferichpublishing.com
1 (844) 686-9607

Because of the dynamic nature of the Internet, any web addresses or links contained in this book may have changed since publication and may no longer be valid. The views expressed in this work are solely those of the author and do not necessarily reflect the views of the publisher, and the publisher hereby disclaims any responsibility for them.

Other books by Reynaldo Encina Jopé:
Feyesper and the Rogue Kite
Feyesper and the Wicked Neighbor

ISBN: 978-1-4897-3095-4 (sc)
ISBN: 978-1-4897-3097-8 (hc)
ISBN: 978-1-4897-3096-1 (e)

Print information available on the last page.

LifeRich Publishing rev. date: 09/16/2020

To

Helen,

Geraldine,

and

Connie

Acknowledgments

When I was in first grade, my teacher, **Mrs. Felipa G. Lacson**, read to our class a story about the pair of slippers a very young **Jose P. Rizal**, the national hero of the Philippines, dropped in the ocean while on board a ship.

My siblings and I grew up watching our father, **Alejandro Jarantilla Jope**, show us what charity really looks like.

Dr. Andrew Engelward, one of my graduate math professors at Harvard University, suggested that I include some mathematics and mathematical thinking in Feyesper's adventure stories.

The first person to inspire me to be an author was **Paquito "Kit" Mandar**. His book, *Flotsammed Years*, an anthology of personal poems, had just come off the press when he became my junior high school English teacher.

These friends of mine took time to read Feyesper's third adventure story before it went to press and offered me valuable feedback and suggestions:

Arnulfo Niñal Leo Lopez Norma Lopez

I thank the **2018 New York City Big Book Awards** for recognizing Feyesper's second adventure story, *Feyesper and the Wicked Neighbor*. It was named a 2018 Distinguished Favorite in the inspirational and motivational categories.

A Note to Parents and Teachers

I am very proud to present Feyesper's third adventure story: *Feyesper and the Red Shoes.*

Like the preceding two books, *Feyesper and the Rogue Kite* (2014) and *Feyesper and the Wicked Neighbor* (2018), *Red Shoes* also entertains and introduces some life lessons. But unlike the first two books, *Red Shoes* mostly teaches about charity.

At the end of the book, you will find a section called **Autosophics.** An integral part of every Feyesper book, this section will equip you with a set of questions to ask your child. Use these questions that beg to be asked to facilitate your child's understanding of what charity is.

As a bonus, this book also presents an opportunity for your child, with your help, to engage in mathematical thinking that is fun and appropriate for your child's age.

Thank you for allowing Feyesper to help create a wiser world for the sweet children in our lives!

Very sincerely yours,

Reynaldo Encina Jopé

It was the last school day before the Christmas break. As had been announced several days earlier, Mr. Chaureau, a barn owl, was now ready to present his students with a numbers puzzle. There was a handsome prize to be won. Close friends and seatmates Picudanny, Oyel, Maty, and Feyesper couldn't wait to play the game. After all, the prize was a store coupon redeemable for a free pair of shoes of one's choice from Sneakers Factory at the local mall.

"The numbers puzzle is revealed in this video," the beloved teacher said to the class. Then, using his phone as a projector, Mr. Chaureau played the video.

The short video featured not one, not two, not three, not four, not five, but *six* charming tarsiers! All of them were excited to play Mr. Chaureau's numbers game.

"Zero!" Faye, the first tarsier, said, feigning surprise.

"One!" Bo, the second tarsier, said with a dab to the left.

"One!" Nat, the third, said with a dab to the right.

"Two!" Shay, the fourth, said with two quick flosses.

"Three!" Zeke, the fifth, said with three squat kicks.

But before Quince, the sixth and last tarsier, could reveal his number, Mr. Chaureau paused the video. Then he asked the class, "What number do you think Quince has, and why?"

The class quickly fell silent, and all students were now engaged in the hunt for Quince's number. Picudanny, a jerboa, counted with his fingers. Feyesper, a pink fairy armadillo or pichiciego, wrote his numbers on air. Oyel, a golden snail, drew sticks on his tablet. Maty, a bantam rooster, drew a number line with hopping curves on a sheet of paper.

In due time, the teacher was happy to announce that everyone could turn in their answers and justifications, but only one student could win the prize.

Norma, who was a pink fairy armadillo like Feyesper, was radiant with happiness and pride when Mr. Chaureau announced her name as the winner of the numbers puzzle and the coveted store coupon.

Unlike his friends, Feyesper wasn't too disappointed. In fact, he was happy that Norma won the coveted prize. Feyesper's admiration for her started on school field day when he saw her play sepak takraw, his favorite Olympic kickball sport. In addition to her sweetness and charm, her kickball abilities were quite impressive.

Feyesper accompanied Norma at Sneakers Factory at the mall to pick the coolest pair of red shoes a girl could ever have. As the store attendant packed her shoes in a colorful bag, Norma twirled as if no one was watching.

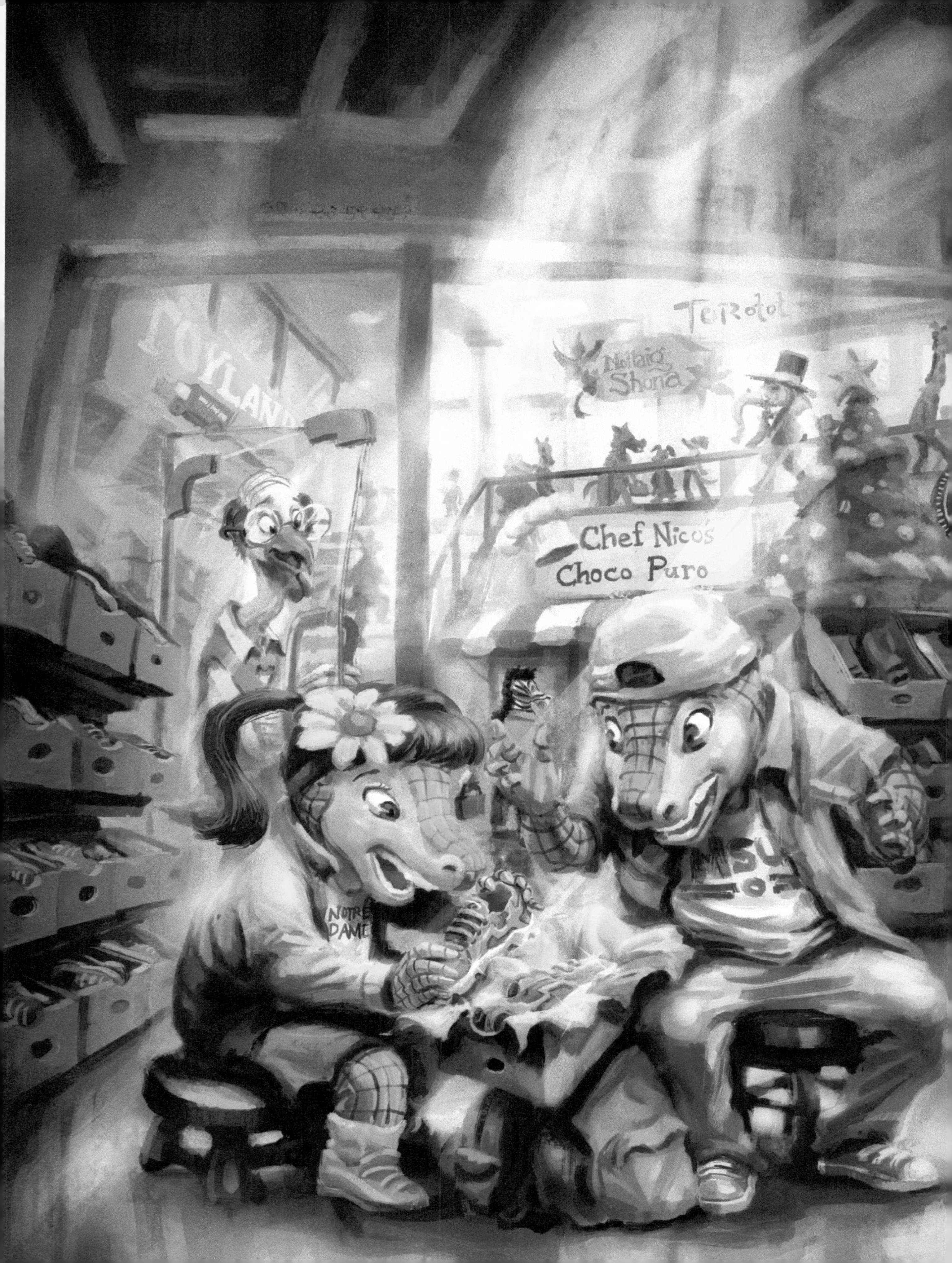
Nollaig Shona
Chef Nico's
Choco Puro
NOTRE DAME

They then enjoyed the elaborate Christmas holiday decorations and festive music that permeated the air inside the mall. They certainly enjoyed the rocky road ice cream cones that they ate as they walked around the mall.

It was all great fun until Norma realized she had lost the bag that contained her red shoes.

"Oh no, my shoes are gone!" Norma said sadly.

"I'll help you find them," Feyesper quickly said.

The two pink fairy armadillos retraced their steps back to every shop they visited. They hoped to find the bag, but it wasn't anywhere they looked.

Now tired and resigned to the fact she might not be able to recover her lost shoes, Norma sadly told Feyesper that she was ready to go home—but not before a quick visit to the restroom.

Just a few feet from the restroom, a mysterious red shoe lay on the floor. Norma saw that it looked just like the ones she had lost. With her heart pounding, she picked up the shoe and went into the restroom.

Inside, a woman who looked upset rushed out of one stall, leaving behind her daughter, who also looked upset. When the woman saw the red shoe that Norma was holding, she was overjoyed.

"Did you drop this?" Norma asked the woman.

The woman paused and then said, "Yes, I did." She then grabbed the red shoe from Norma's outstretched hand and quickly turned around to join her daughter back in the stall.

Stunned by what had happened, Norma could see below the closed stall door a pair of dirty shoes being replaced by a pair of brand-new, shiny red ones. There were no signs of the shoebox and the colorful bag around.

A few minutes later, Norma heard the woman quietly say, "Merry Christmas, my sweet child!"

Norma had joined Feyesper a short distance from the restroom when the woman and her daughter, who was now wearing the red shoes, briskly walked by. To Feyesper, the daughter looked as if she had just won some coveted prize in a fun game like Mr. Chaureau's. She hopped like there were puddles of water to jump over along the way.

Norma studied the paper receipt she received from the shoe store one more time. Then she crumpled it up and dropped it in the recycling bin. When she looked up, the mother and daughter were gone.

"Those red shoes belong to her," Norma told Feyesper. "They are her Christmas present."

As the two pink fairy armadillos headed out of the mall, Feyesper was pleased to see that Norma wasn't sad anymore.

At dinnertime, Feyesper told his mom, Mrs. Ayebeeb, all that happened at the mall. She listened to her beloved son. When Feyesper finished, she put an arm around him and said, "Norma may have lost her shoes altogether, but like Cinderella, she is going to be a queen."

AUTOSOPHICS[1]

1. Have you seen or heard about homeless people?

2. What do you know about homeless people?

3. How do you compare homeless people to yourself?

4. Do homeless people live happily or sadly?

5. How do you think they survive?

6. If you meet a homeless person on the street and that person is hungry, what should you do? Should you just ignore them?

7. Should you buy them food?

8. Would you prefer to just give them money instead of buying them food?

9. When Norma found a red shoe outside the restroom, what do you think was she thinking?

---

[1] I coined the term *Autosophics* from *auto*, self, and *sophos*, wisdom.

10. When she went inside the restroom, what do you think was she hoping would happen?

11. What two people did she meet inside the restroom?

12. The lady was happy to see the red shoe Norma was holding. If you were Norma, would you give her the shoe?

13. What did the lady tell her daughter when she finally got the red shoes on?

14. On their way out of the mall, the girl with the red shoes "hopped like there were puddles of water to jump over." What did that mean?

15. When Norma told Feyesper that the red shoes belonged to her, what do you think she was thinking at that moment?

16. Read this word out loud: *charity*.

17. Now spell *charity* loudly.

18. When you help homeless people or anybody in need, what do you think it is called?

19. Did Norma give away her new red shoes?

20. Did Norma do an act of charity at the mall? Why or why not?

21. When Feyesper came home, his mom, Mrs. Ayebeeb, said, "Norma may have lost her shoes altogether, but like Cinderella, she is going to be a queen." What did she mean by that?

22. If you were Norma, would you have done anything differently? Why?

23. What do you think charity is?

24. Is it important that all people in the world do acts of charity frequently?

25. What if nobody ever did any acts of charity for people in need?

26. Do you plan to do acts of charity for others?

SUGGESTED ACTIVITY #1

Write down the following five digits,

followed by two empty spaces:

0, 1, 1, 2, 3, ___, ___, ...

Ask your child to read the digits out loud.

Then ask, "What digits would best fill the two

empty spaces? Why do you think so?"

Allow your child to express their thoughts freely. Express your own thoughts freely too. Make sure that it is about thinking and expressing oneself freely and not just about arriving at some right answers. Mathematical thinking doesn't have to end with a right answer.

SUGGESTED ACTIVITY #2

For more fun, search and read

about the following online:

Fibonacci sequence

SUGGESTED ACTIVITY #3

Create your own Fibonacci sequence.

Yes, you can!

Start with any two numbers that you like. Then figure out the next five numbers. If you like, you may ask someone else to write out your Fibonacci sequence.

Have fun with your Fibonacci sequence!

Lightning Source UK Ltd.
Milton Keynes UK
UKHW051306011020
370839UK00006B/85